DANGER
AT SAND CAVE

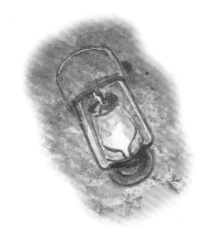

DANGER
AT SAND CAVE

by Candice F. Ransom
illustrations by Den Schofield

M Millbrook Press / Minneapolis

For my good friend Brad—C.F.R.

I'd like to dedicate this book to my young friend Grahame Wilson, who did such a fine job modeling for the character Arly in this story—D.S.

Text copyright © 2000 by Candice F. Ransom
Illustrations copyright © 2000 by Den Schofield

This book is available in two editions:
Library binding by Millbrook Press, a division of Lerner Publishing Group, Inc.
Soft cover by First Avenue Editions, an imprint of Lerner Publishing Group, Inc.
241 First Avenue North
Minneapolis, MN 55401 U.S.A.

Website address: www.lernerbooks.com

Library of Congress Cataloging-in-Publication Data

Ransom, Candice F., 1952–
     Danger at Sand Cave / by Candice F. Ransom ; illustrations by Den
  Schofield.
        p. cm. — (On my own history)
     Summary: When his friend, Floyd Collins, becomes trapped in a cave
  in Kentucky in 1925, ten-year-old Arly places himself in great
  danger while trying to help with the rescue operation.
     ISBN 978–1–57505–379–0 (lib. bdg. : alk. paper)
     ISBN 978–1–57505–454–4 (pbk. : alk. paper)
     ISBN 978–1–57505–559–6 (eBook)
     [1. Rescue work—Fiction. 2. Caves—Fiction. 3. Collins, Floyd,
  1890–1925—Fiction.] I. Schofield, Den, ill. II. Title.
  III. Series.
  PZ7.R1743Dan   2000
  [B]–dc21   99–21416

Manufactured in the United States of America
8 – PC – 4/1/13

Author's Note

On January 30, 1925, a man crawled into a cavern called Sand Cave. The man's name was Floyd Collins. At thirty-seven, Floyd was used to exploring caves. Cave City, his home in central Kentucky, was riddled with underground caverns.

That cold Friday night, Floyd slithered into Sand Cave's narrow tunnel. He carried only a kerosene lantern and a length of rope. He wriggled and squeezed until he was fifty-five feet from the entrance. Suddenly, his lantern tipped over and went out. Floyd kicked against a limestone rock. Part of the rock fell on his left foot. Then a shower of rocks and dirt fell on his legs, covering them.

Floyd was trapped.

The next day, Floyd's neighbors and relatives found him. But no one could free him. The tunnel was too small for anyone to dig him out.

This is the story of what happened at Sand Cave. Ten-year-old Arly Dunbar is not a real person. But the plight of Floyd Collins is true.

Cave City, Kentucky
Thursday, February 5, 1925

Arly Dunbar stared at the soldiers.
They stood in front of him, holding guns.
Floyd Collins had been trapped
in Sand Cave for six days.
Many people had come to help.
Others just wanted to watch.
The soldiers were blocking the cave
to keep the people out.

Arly and his cousin Russell
were at Sand Cave to help.
Floyd was their friend.
Once, Arly and Russell had visited him
at Crystal Cave.
Crystal Cave was a cavern Floyd owned.

Floyd showed them rock crystals
shaped like flowers.
He gave Arly one to keep.
That day, Arly became a caver,
just like Floyd and Russell.

"Arly," a voice said. It was Russell.

"How about some coffee for the diggers?"

The diggers were some of the men

who were trying to save Floyd.

Russell was one of them.

They were digging a shaft

so they could get Floyd out.

Arly had been staying
with the diggers, running errands.
"Okay," he told Russell.
Quickly he ran to fetch the coffee.

11

As he ran, Arly thought about Russell.

He was the bravest person Arly knew.

A few days ago,

Russell had crawled into Sand Cave.

He brought food and water to Floyd.

Other men had visited Floyd, too.

But as they crawled down the tunnel,

they rubbed against the ceiling.

The ceiling got weaker.

Finally, part of it caved in.

Floyd was shut off from the world.

No one could clear away

the rocks that blocked the tunnel.

"It's like digging in a barrel of apples,"

Russell had told Arly.

Arly understood.

The loose rocks shifted.

If you moved one, fifty fell in its place.

That was why the men

decided to dig a shaft.

This shaft was next to Floyd's tunnel.

Maybe they could reach Floyd that way.

Arly brought the coffee
to the diggers' tent.
A crew had just finished their shift.
Their faces were streaked with mud.

16

The men dropped onto cots
without changing their dirty clothes.
Arly pulled off a digger's boots.
"Thanks," the man said.
Then he fell asleep.

Arly quietly left the tent.

It was warm for early February.

The frozen ground was thawing.

Water might flood the shaft.

The men would have to dig even harder.

Arly stopped again at the cave's entrance.

Floyd had been trapped for nearly a week.

When would he be freed?

Arly wished he could do

more than fetch coffee.

If only *he* could free his friend.

Early Sunday morning,

Arly lifted the tent flap.

He couldn't believe his eyes.

Thousands of people mobbed the fields!

Each day had brought more people,

but nothing like this.

Cars clogged the muddy road.

Wagons sold hot dogs and soda pop.

Children held balloons

that said SAND CAVE.

Reporters called their newspapers
from telephones nailed to trees.
It was like the county fair!
"Crazy city folks!" said Russell.
"They can't get near Floyd."
Arly nodded.
"Floyd wanted folks to visit his caves.
But he'd never want all this!" he said.

That night, it rained.

Water flooded the shaft.

Then it began to snow.

Arly took blankets

to the freezing rescue workers.

He ran back and forth with hot drinks.

He helped diggers tug off muddy overalls.

22

Hours and days dragged by.

Floyd had been trapped for thirteen days.

He had not eaten for a week.

Arly felt guilty

when he ate supper in the mess tent.

The next day was Friday, February 13.
Arly brought the diggers their mail.
"Tomorrow is Valentine's Day,"
said Russell.
"Arly, can you get us some red paper?"

"Can't I help dig?" Arly asked.

"We don't want you to get hurt,"

said Russell.

Arly walked away.

Would he ever get to help Floyd?

Arly went to town.

He bought red paper at the store.

When he got back,

everyone was excited.

"One of the diggers heard Floyd cough!"

Russell told him.

The workers still hadn't broken

into Floyd's tunnel.

But they must be close, Arly thought.

And if Floyd had coughed,

he was still alive!

Reporters raced to their phones

to call in the news flash.

But a while later, the shaft's walls fell in.

The diggers would have to start over.

Saturday began with rain and fog.

The workers were glum.

But it was Valentine's Day.

The crews gave paper hearts

to each other.

Then they went to work.

They wouldn't give up

until they reached Floyd.

Alone in the tent, Arly had an idea.

No one had talked to Floyd for days.

Arly cut out a red heart and wrote,

To Floyd, from your friend Arly.

He tied his crystal flower to the heart.

Floyd was sealed behind a wall of rock.

But maybe Arly could get through.

He was small.

He could help his friend.

Arly picked up a lantern
and walked to the cave.
The soldiers were talking.
They looked tired.
They didn't see Arly sneak
through the barbed wire.
He quickly slipped into Sand Cave.

At first, Arly could walk.

Soon he had to stoop, then crawl.

The light grew dimmer.

Arly turned on his lantern.

Headfirst, he slid down the tunnel.

Sharp rocks scraped his elbows.

He felt icy water under his arms.

He slid through freezing mud.

The passage kept getting smaller.

At one spot, it was only ten inches wide.

Arly pushed his lantern past the hole.

Then he forced his head through.

His ears were skinned raw.

Arly squeezed his shoulders past the rock
and pulled his legs through.

The cave opened into a room.

Arly could sit up.

The tunnel kept going down.

His feet dangled into the chute below.

He stopped to catch his breath.

In the lantern's light,

cave crickets hopped from rock to rock.

Arly heard his heart pound.

No wonder the rescuers

had never stayed with Floyd for long.

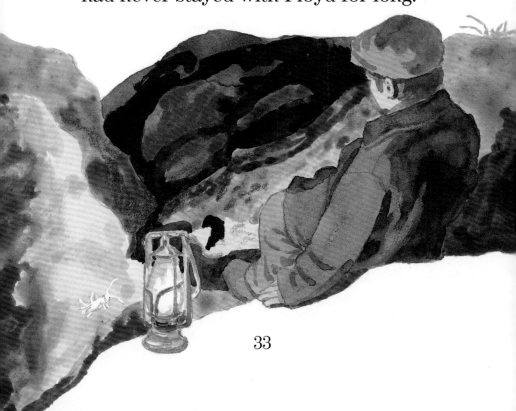

With a gulp,

Arly eased his way down the chute.

Soon he reached a pile of loose limestone.

Floyd lay just past this fallen rock.

"Floyd?" Arly whispered.

His voice sounded loud.

"Floyd!" he called. "It's me, Arly Dunbar."

No answer.

"I brought you something," Arly said.
"It's a Valentine's heart.
Everybody is working real hard
to get you out, Floyd."

Arly pulled the heart from his pocket.

His hand knocked against the rocks.

Frightened, Arly dropped the lantern.

Suddenly, he was in total darkness!

Arly gasped in panic.

No one knew he was down here.

Not even Russell.

And no one would come down.

It was too dangerous.

How could he have been so dumb?

He and Floyd were *both* trapped!

Russell had always said

cavers should explore with a buddy.

If one got hurt, the buddy could get help.

Then Arly remembered something else.

When he visited Crystal Cave,

Floyd had turned off the lights.

He led Arly through the dark cavern.

Floyd had told him to feel his way out.

Arly felt the space around him.

It hadn't changed.

He just couldn't see it.

Arly took deep breaths.

Slowly, his fear eased.

He had climbed down this hole.

He would get out again.

Arly began backing up the tunnel.

Gripping with his toes,

he pushed himself along.

Soon he saw a glimmer of light.

Arly sighed with relief.

"Floyd!" he called one more time.

Still no answer.

"I'm real sorry, Floyd," Arly said.

"I wish I could help."

Then he turned and kept crawling.

When Arly came out of Sand Cave,

a soldier spotted him.

Then Russell rushed forward.

"It's okay. He's my cousin," Russell said.

The soldier let them go.

"What were you doing?" Russell asked.

"You could have been killed!"

"I wanted to help," Arly said.

"I thought I could talk to Floyd.

Ask him how he's doing."

"You are helping," Russell told him.

"You bring the men coffee.

You fetch the newspapers and mail."

"That's nothing," Arly said.

"It is something," Russell argued.

"Every man counts here."

But Arly still felt bad.

He had failed to save Floyd.

On Monday,

the diggers broke into Floyd's tunnel.

Everyone shouted with joy.

But Floyd Collins was dead.

Arly cried.

He remembered Floyd

proudly showing Crystal Cave to visitors.

"Why did Floyd have to die?"

he asked Russell.

"We just couldn't get to him in time,"

Russell said.

"If only I could have helped," Arly said.

"You did," said Russell. "We all did."

Arly shook his head.

"All I did was get in trouble," he said.

"But I'm not going to quit caving."

He knew Floyd wouldn't want him to.

"Me neither," said Russell.

"But don't go caving alone, Arly.

Come with me."

"Really?" Arly was amazed.

"You're a good caver," said Russell.

"You don't panic."

The next day, Arly and Russell
went to a service for Floyd.
Newspapermen snapped photos
of Floyd's family.
Pastors gave sermons.
Arly remembered how Floyd
loved caving more than anything.

Arly started to feel a little better.
He knew that he and Russell
would never forget Floyd Collins.
And they would never forget
the bravery of the workers
who tried so hard to save him.